PUMPKIN SMILE

PUMPKIN SMILE

EMILY CHETKOWSKI
ILLUSTRATED BY DAWN PETERSON

SEVEN COIN PRESS
SPRUCE HEAD, MAINE

SEVEN COIN PRESS

P.O. Box 477 • Spruce Head, Maine 04859
Phone: 207-594-0906 • www.sevencoinpress.com

ISBN 0-9700974-2-5
ISBN 0-9700974-3-3 (pbk.)

Printed and bound in China through Regent Publishing Services, New York
01 02 03 04 05 10 9 8 7 6 5 4 3 2 1

At first they got wiggly,
but then they got wobbly,
and then they fell out one by one.

Big gaps and wide spaces,
no teeth in their places,
the Tooth Fairy's visits were fun.

Hannah thought it was great
then noticed the gape,
as well as her tongue sticking through.

"I look kind of thilly.
I don't thound the thame.
Oh, what did that Toof Fairy do?"

Hannah still was a cutie,
and really a beauty,
but she didn't think so at all.

Her mom said, "It's slow,
but the new ones will grow,
you should have them, I think, by the fall."

"I know what I'll do!
My tongue won't thick through
if I never thmile anymore!"

Then she closed her mouth tight.
No teeth were in sight,
until they would look like before.

No smiles at the jokes
she heard from her folks.
She claimed that the jokes were all bad.

She just didn't buckle
with even a chuckle.
Instead she would look rather sad.

The fall leaves got wiggly,
and then they got wobbly.
They fell off the trees one by one.

With branches all bare
and frost everywhere,
the time came for Halloween fun.

Hannah thought it was great,
then looked at the gape,
and saw her tongue *still* sticking through.

"Well, isn't this thomething,
I look like a pumpkin!
Oh, what in the world will I do?"

For Halloween night,
with candles so bright,
Jack O'Lanterns were real works of art.

The one that was best
would win a contest,
but Hannah refused to take part.

No idea could she find
for her pumpkin design
till Dad said, "I know what we'll do."

"Come sit for a while
and show me that smile.
We'll carve it to look just like you."

Now slowly she brightened,
her sweet face untightened.
She grinned a big grin ear-to-ear.

Then quickly they worked
to carve out that smirk
in time for the contest so near.

The bonfire that night
was such a delight.
Hannah's pumpkin had won by a mile.

But she knew the best,
above all the rest,
was really her *own* pumpkin smile!

THE END

About the Author

Children's author **Emily Chetkowski** is best known for the classic New England favorites, *Mabel Takes the Ferry* and *Mabel Takes a Sail*. She and her family live in Massachusetts on a small farm with an assortment of appealing animals and spend the summer on a Maine island, where she does most of her writing. Emily's other well-known titles include *Amasa Walker's Splendid Garment* and *Gooseman*.

About the Illustrator

Freelance illustrator **Dawn Peterson** has illustrated many children's books, including *Mabel Takes the Ferry, Mabel Takes a Sail, Orphan Seal, Miss Renee's Mice,* and the *L. L. Bear* series of books. Dawn lives with her comical cat, Houda, on the coast of Maine near her two daughters and their families.